Hi, I'm JIMMY!

Like me, you probably noticed the world is run by adults.

But ask yourself: Who would do the best job

of making books that *kids* will love?

Yeah. **Kids!**

So that's how the idea of JIMMY books came to life.

We want every JIMMY book to be so good

that when you're finished, you'll say,

"PLEASE GIVE ME ANOTHER BOOK!"

Give this one a try and see if you agree.

(If not, you're probably an adult!)

JIMMY PATTERSON BOOKS
FOR YOUNG READERS

James Patterson Presents

Sci-Fi Junior High by John Martin and Scott Seegert

Sci-Fi Junior High: Crash Landing by John Martin and Scott Seegert

How to Be a Supervillain by Michael Fry

How to Be a Supervillain: Born to Be Good by Michael Fry

How to Be a Supervillain: Bad Guys Finish First by Michael Fry

The Unflushables by Ron Bates

Ernestine, Catastrophe Queen by Merrill Wyatt

Scouts by Shannon Greenland

The Middle School Series by James Patterson

Middle School, The Worst Years of My Life

Middle School: Get Me Out of Here!

Middle School: Big Fat Liar

Middle School: How I Survived Bullies, Broccoli, and Snake Hill

Middle School: Ultimate Showdown

Middle School: Save Rafe!

Middle School: Just My Rotten Luck

Middle School: Dog's Best Friend

Middle School: Escape to Australia

Middle School: From Hero to Zero

Middle School: Born to Rock

Middle School: Master of Disaster

The I Funny Series by James Patterson

I Funny

I Even Funnier

I Totally Funniest

I Funny TV

I Funny: School of Laughs

The Nerdiest, Wimpiest, Dorkiest I Funny Ever

The Treasure Hunters Series by James Patterson

Treasure Hunters

Treasure Hunters: Danger Down the Nile

Treasure Hunters: Secret of the Forbidden City

Treasure Hunters: Peril at the Top of the World

Treasure Hunters: Quest for the City of Gold

Treasure Hunters: All-American Adventure

The House of Robots Series by James Patterson

House of Robots

House of Robots: Robots Go Wild!

House of Robots: Robot Revolution

The Daniel X Series by James Patterson

The Dangerous Days of Daniel X
Daniel X: Watch the Skies
Daniel X: Demons and Druids
Daniel X: Game Over
Daniel X: Armageddon
Daniel X: Lights Out

Other Illustrated Novels and Stories

Ali Cross
Katt Vs. Dogg
Dog Diaries
Dog Diaries: Happy Howlidays
Max Einstein: The Genius Experiment
Max Einstein: Rebels with a Cause
Unbelievably Boring Bart
Not So Normal Norbert
Laugh Out Loud
Pottymouth and Stoopid
Jacky Ha-Ha
Jacky Ha-Ha: My Life Is a Joke
Public School Superhero
Word of Mouse
Give Please a Chance
Give Thank You a Try
Big Words for Little Geniuses
Bigger Words for Little Geniuses
Cuddly Critters for Little Geniuses
The Candies Save Christmas

For exclusives, trailers, and other information, visit jimmypatterson.org.

To my dearest dad: love always. —B.T.

Copyright © 2020 by James Patterson
Illustrations by Betty C. Tang

JIMMY Patterson Books / Little, Brown and Company
Hachette Book Group
1290 Avenue of the Americas, New York, NY 10104
JamesPatterson.com

First Graphic Novel Edition: May 2020

JIMMY Patterson Books is an imprint of Little, Brown and Company, a division of Hachette Book Group, Inc. The Little, Brown name and logo are trademarks of Hachette Book Group, Inc. The JIMMY Patterson Books® name and logo are trademarks of JBP Business, LLC.

ISBN 978-0-316-49195-2

Library of Congress Control Number 2019957380

10 9 8 7 6 5 4 3 2 1

Printed in China

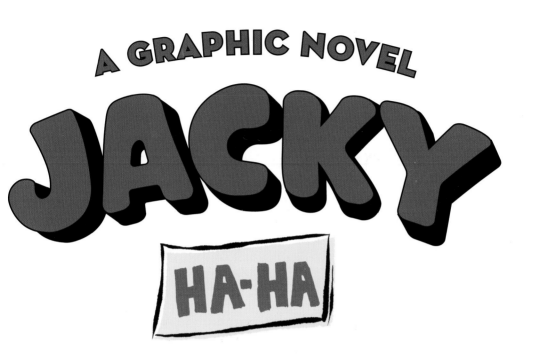

A GRAPHIC NOVEL

JACKY

HA-HA

JAMES PATTERSON
AND CHRIS GRABENSTEIN

ADAPTED BY ADAM RAU
ILLUSTRATED BY BETTY C. TANG

jimmy
patterson

JIMMY PATTERSON BOOKS
LITTLE, BROWN AND COMPANY
NEW YORK BOSTON LONDON

It starts when I decided—in the middle of the night!—to climb up to the top of the Ferris wheel on the Seaside Heights boardwalk in New Jersey.

So here it is, ladies—the funny, the not-so-funny, and the embarrassingly true story of the year that changed my life.

9

11

18

Our father, Mac Hart, is the captain of the Seaside Heights Beach Patrol. That means he's the head lifeguard.

It also means he's a total hunk.

My mom even had a special T-shirt printed for him when they were first dating.

Woo!

Ahh

Mmm

Seaside Heights Beach Patrol

BEST Looking boy on the beach

Seriously.

What happened?

W-w-we ate too much?

And whose idea was that?

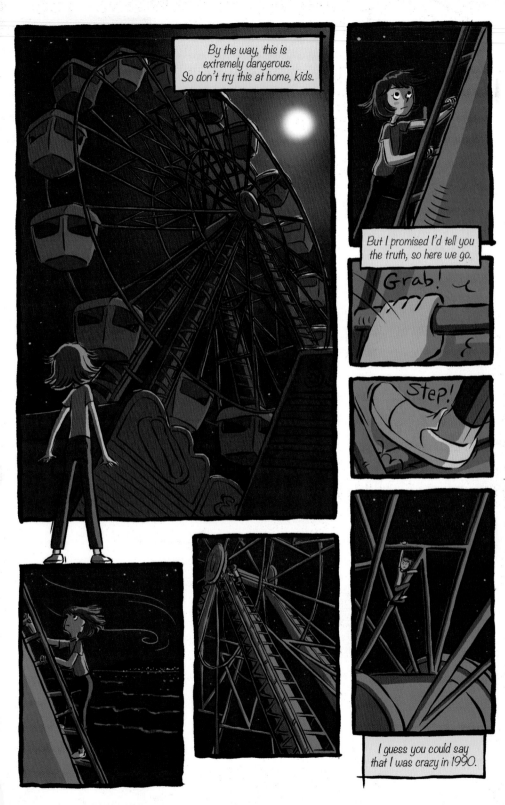

23

And fearless.

And a little foolish.

Whew!

I am doing this insane thing tonight, because tomorrow I'm going to start a sane year at school.

I'm going to stop being the class clown.

I'm also going to write more letters to Mom in Saudi Arabia, visit Nonna in her nursing home more often, and be nicer to Dad and my sisters, especially Riley.

I'm going to be a new me. No more Jacky Ha-Ha! This I do solemnly swear!

26

27

28

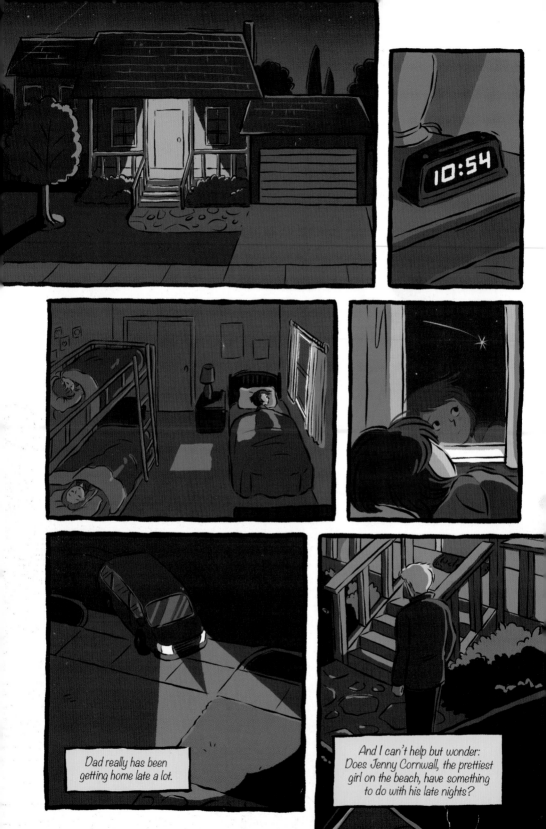

Dad really has been getting home late a lot.

And I can't help but wonder: Does Jenny Cornwall, the prettiest girl on the beach, have something to do with his late nights?

42

45

48

Dear Jacky,

Life as a staff sergeant in the Air Control Group of the Marine Corps is about as exciting as you could expect. Lots of planes need to take off and land safely, and I make sure everything goes smoothly.

You wouldn't believe how hot it is here! The bus ride that takes us from the control tower to the base is thirty minutes of sweltering heat. Even on full blast, the air conditioners don't do a thing! It's one hundred and twenty-seven degrees in the shade, except there's absolutely no shade. Just sand. (I included some for your growing collection of beach sand. Now you have some sand from halfway around the world!) To see how hot it is here, put it in the microwave for about forty-five seconds. On the other hand, don't. In fact, forget I even wrote that!

I miss you guys like crazy, and I don't want you worrying about me. We're miles away from any real fighting that takes place. The bad news is, we don't know when Uncle Sam will send us home. The good news? I've already picked out my Halloween costume for next year.

I love you so much!

Mom

P.S. Help your sisters and Dad as much as possible while I'm gone.

67

79

83

That Sunday, we go to church.

Jacky. You know I want you to wear your best clothes to church.

I hate dresses. You can't win a bike race in a dress.

Go change.

Okay.

Lord, it's me, Jacky. From the Ferris wheel? Please protect my mom the way she protects everybody else. Bless her and bring her home.

I need her. We all do. But to be totally honest, I think I might need her a little more than everybody else.

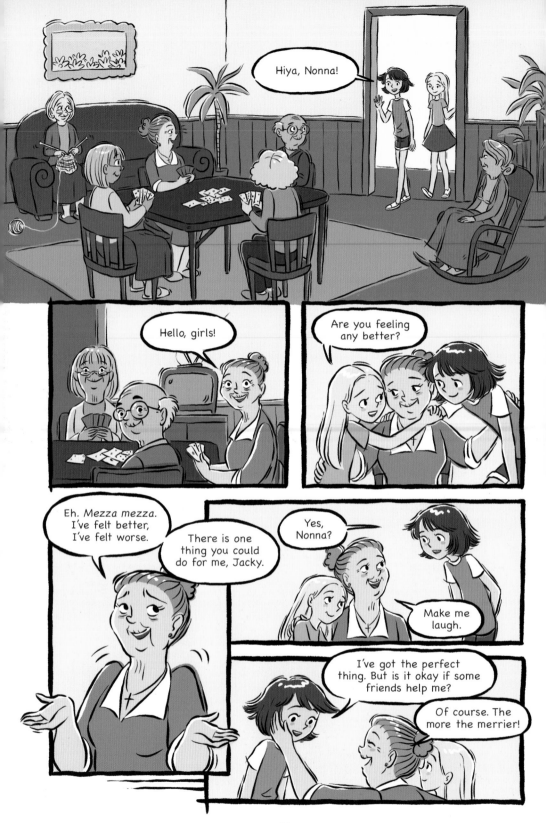

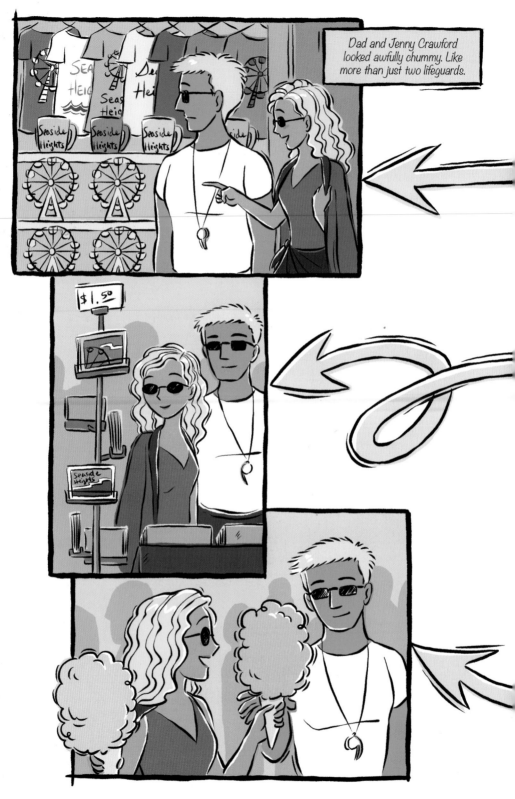

Toms River

Seaside Heights

Lacey Township

Long Beach Island

Beach Haven

Atlantic City

Ocean City

CRAZY MOUSE

The best thing about any boardwalk is the buskers, which is another word for street performers.

Good thing I brought my lunch box.

Drop

What are you doing?

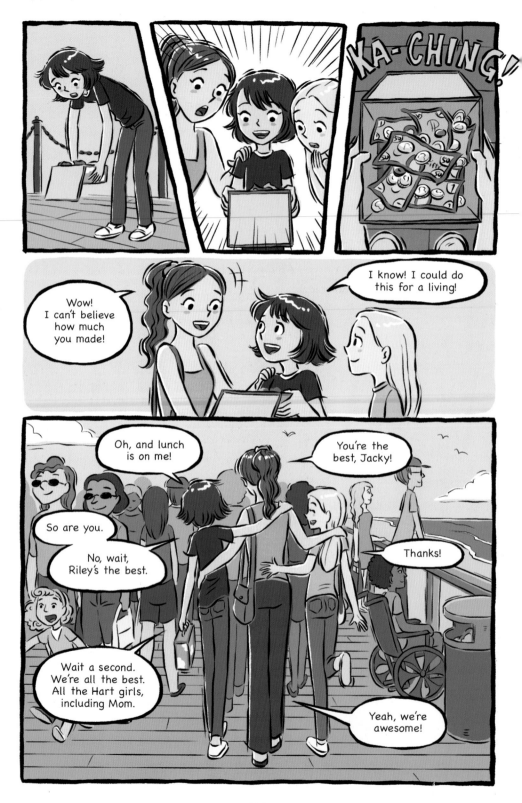

So I write the letter I'll actually send.

Dear Mom,
How are
we're g

It's a very Jacky Ha-Ha letter.

128

134

Everything's easier the second time you do it.

So I figured it was time to climb to the top of the Ferris wheel and make another solemn vow.

143

145

A-113

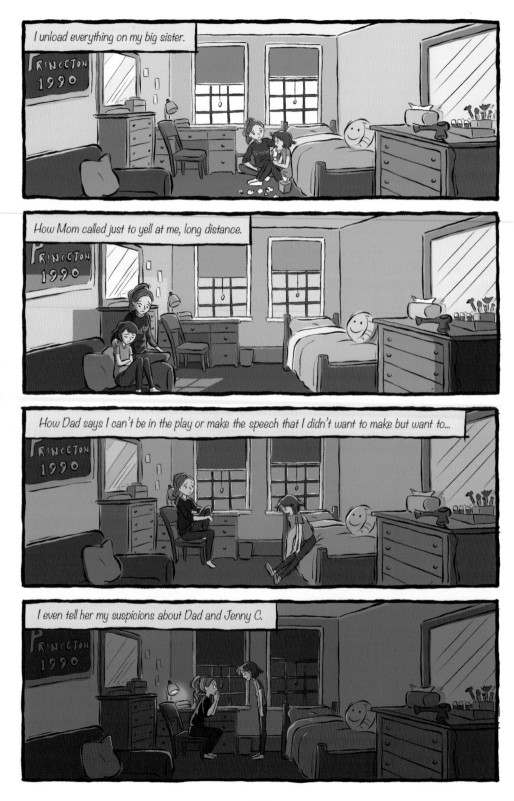

157

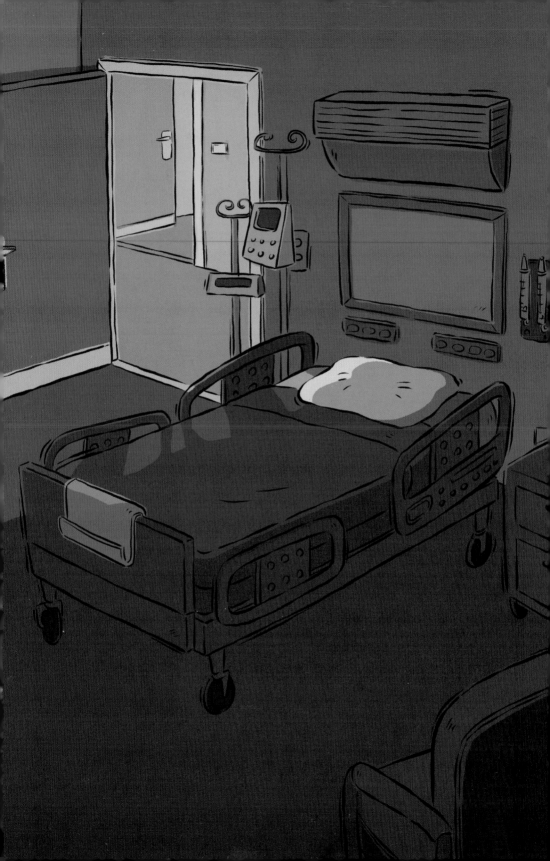

Because it's what she always told me to do! "Make me laugh, Jacky. Make me laugh."

Those were practically her dying words to me...

BEEEEP!

Okay, Jacky. Make your speech. Do the play. Make your Nonna laugh. I guess we could all use a laugh this week.

I'll see you later.

The next couple of afternoons are eaten up by Charlie Brown tech rehearsals and costume fittings.

173

174

All those citizen soldiers who are now in harm's way, standing guard on a wall or huddled in the desert, or soaring across the sky—all of them out there defending our Constitution.
These Americans surely know their duty to their country, because they live that duty every day. They also stand as a shining beacon of inspiration, showing us how we can choose to live our lives.
How we can all choose to serve something bigger than ourselves. Something more important. We can all make the same kind of vow to do our duty, whatever that duty might be.
Because it is only in so swearing and so doing that those of us living in this wonderful country can secure the blessings of liberty for ourselves and our posterity, which, by the way, means "our children and all their children."
What Mom has done for me, I hope to someday do for others. Maybe in the Marines or the other armed services, or maybe not. But I will listen for my calling, find my duty, and then I will do it, so help me God.

...m-m-much.

TAKE YOUR TIME

This was the day I first learned the true meaning of the old adage "The show must go on."

No matter what tragedies are going on in your personal life, if you are in a play or doing a TV show, the audience wants to be entertained...

...not see you bawl buckets of tears because your beloved grandmother passed away.

That was good, what you said. The speech at the school. And then today. The joke. At the funeral.

Thank you?

These last few weeks have been rough, Jacky. For all of us. It's good to have your mom home.

Anyway, tonight's your big night. Meredith says I'm supposed to say "Break a leg." I don't really know why.

It's just another way of saying "good luck."

Really?

What can I tell you? Theater people are weird. Which is maybe why I blend in so well with them.

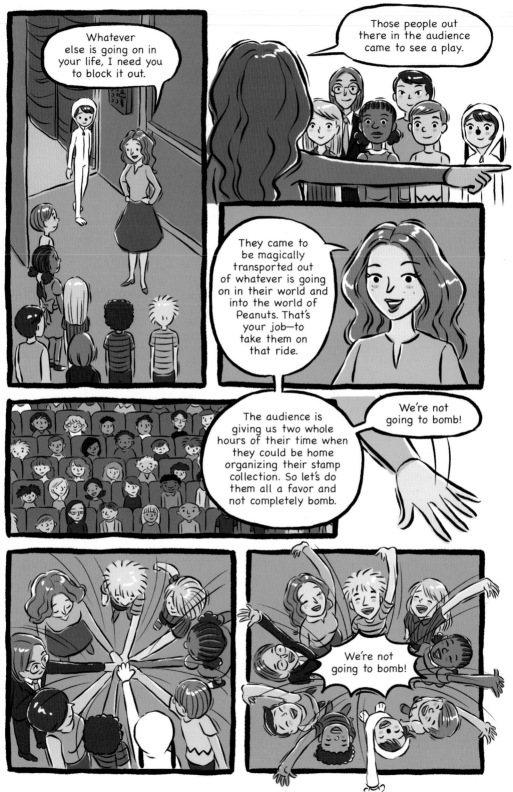

Later.

So, who lives here?

Friend of the family. I want to introduce you.

DING DONG

This is where your humble narrator, your mom, admits something I know you two girls will find extremely hard to believe: Sometimes I make mistakes.

First of all I want to thank the people who first called what I had *talent* instead of what everybody else called it: *trouble*. Ms. O'Mara and Mrs. Turner. Two amazing women from my middle school in Seaside Heights.

Of course I need to thank my director, my cowriters, our cast and crew. You guys were my on-set family, and I love you all.

And let's not forget my best friend since forever, Meredith Crawford. Thank you for singing our title song for us...and congratulations on your Oscar tonight, too.

Our Oscars will also be best friends!

Finally, and most important, I want to thank my real family. My six incredible sisters, who are the best friends a girl could ever wish for. And our mother and father, who taught us that there's always something in the world much more important than ourselves.

ABOUT THE AUTHORS

JAMES PATTERSON received the Literarian Award for Outstanding Service to the American Literary Community from the National Book Foundation. He holds the Guinness World Record for the most #1 *New York Times* bestsellers, including *Max Einstein, Middle School, I Funny*, and *Jacky Ha-Ha*, and his books have sold more than 385 million copies worldwide. A tireless champion of the power of books and reading, Patterson created a children's book imprint, JIMMY Patterson, whose mission is simple: "We want every kid who finishes a JIMMY Book to say, 'PLEASE GIVE ME ANOTHER BOOK.'" He has donated more than three million books to students and soldiers and funds over four hundred Teacher and Writer Education Scholarships at twenty-one colleges and universities. He has also donated millions of dollars to independent bookstores and school libraries. Patterson invests proceeds from the sales of JIMMY Patterson Books in pro-reading initiatives.

CHRIS GRABENSTEIN is a *New York Times* bestselling author who has collaborated with James Patterson on the Max Einstein, I Funny, Jacky Ha-Ha, Treasure Hunters, and House of Robots series, as well as *Word of Mouse, Katt vs. Dogg, Pottymouth and Stoopid, Laugh Out Loud*, and *Daniel X: Armageddon*. He lives in New York City.

ADAM RAU was born in Minnesota and moved to New York to attend The School of Visual Arts. In 2004 he landed a job in children's publishing, and before long he was acquiring and editing graphic novels for young readers, which he has been doing for over ten years. Adam lives in Jersey City with his wife and dog.

BETTY C. TANG has been in the animation and illustration world for more than twenty-five years. She has worked for acclaimed studios including DreamWorks Animation and Disney Television Animation, co-directed the Chinese animated feature film, *Where's the Dragon?*, and illustrated for books and magazines. Born in Taiwan, she now lives in Los Angeles, California and writes and illustrates for children.

5